By Golly, Molly, You're Right

Bobby Hawley

PublishAmerica
Baltimore

First printing

At the specific preference of the author, PublishAmerica allowed this work to remain exactly as the author intended, verbatim, without editorial input.

ISBN: 1-4241-2085-3
PUBLISHED BY PUBLISHAMERICA, LLLP
www.publishamerica.com
Baltimore

Printed in the United States of America

DEDICATION

To all the children who have been bullied, I hope you can find the strength to rise above your fears and become your own hero.

To my mother who was always ready and willing to help those in need.

ACKNOWLEDGEMENTS

A special thanks to a very generous friend, Barbara Moore. She was always available when I required her help with a problem, or someone just to listen.

Craig Roberts, an experienced animator, did the illustrations. Good illustrations breathe life into the text. Thanks Craig!

INTRODUCTION

Fear

I lay awake
In my bed at night
Pulling the covers
Around me tight.
Once there were monsters
I used to dread
In my closet
And under my bed.
Late at night,
When the lights went out,
That's when I'd hear them
Scurrying about.
I had nightmares
That filled me with fear,
So Mommy and Daddy
Had to be near.
My bedroom monsters
Have faded away.
I know now
Why they didn't stay.
They were imaginary,
They weren't real
But when your little

It's how you feel.
Now there are monsters
In the light of day,
They're in the classroom
And schoolyard at play.
I try to ignore them
But deep inside
I want to be invisible
Or run and hide.
The monsters come near
But are they real?
Do they sense my fear
And the way I feel?
Does my fear
Create the monsters
That I see?
Or do the monsters
Create the fear
Inside of me?

To Jessica:…
Empathy

Did you see the girl
In the corner cry?
Did you feel her pain?
Did you know she's shy?
Did you comfort her?
Did you find out why?
Did you even care
That her heart was broken
From things that were done
And words that were spoken?

It was a fresh September morning and all the schools lay empty and waiting. The classrooms were bright and cheery, presenting a warm and welcoming atmosphere. Soon the stillness would be shattered by the energy of the young.

"Hurry up Molly! You don't want to be late the first day at your new school," called Mom, from the bottom of the stairs.

Molly cringed at the sound of "new school."

"Where could I hide that I'd never be found? Under the bed, in the closet, maybe up in the attic? There's no escape!" lamented Molly. "They'll find me, wherever I am."

The thought of another new school was frightening because of the many, painful past memories that filled her head and saddened her heart. She had never talked to her mother or father about what was happening in the classroom or on the playground for fear they'd contact the school. She kept her feelings buried, deep inside. They thought her experiences at school were like every other child's. In their wildest dreams, they never would have imagined a day made up of rejections, taunting and sometimes pushing or poking. Molly feared that if she complained to anyone, she'd be labeled a tattletale or a snitch, which would make her life even more unbearable, if that were possible.

Molly sat on the edge of her bed with her hands folded in her lap and her head down. She was the picture of rejection.

"I remember when I first started to feel this way," thought Molly. "It was when mom used to drop me off at the daycare when I was three. At first I thought it was a terrific place to be. All those kids to play with, lots of toys, books, big building blocks, a perfect outdoor play area with slides and a great jungle gym. I never felt shy then. I was happy and could hardly wait to get there to play with the other kids. Then this woman came to work for the daycare and she had a daughter, Margaret, who came with her. Margaret was very selfish and hated sharing. Most kids that age are like that. Her mother gave her all the attention and accused others of being mean to Margaret. There were days when I fought with Margaret and her mother blamed me for starting everything. It wasn't true! Everyday she sat me in a corner for time out and forgot all about me. Sometimes she would say, as she sent me to the corner, 'You're not a very nice little girl!' Other times she would say, 'You're a mean and spoiled child!' Her voice sounded harsh and nasty like an old witch and her eyes showed her dislike...I'll never forget her! There were days she even called me stupid. She made sure that no one else heard these abuses. I did a lot of crying and some mornings I refused to return. I hated that daycare! Mom made me go back because this woman assured her that it was just a stage I was going through. From then on I kept quiet and never joined in any of the activities. I prayed to become invisible. This woman filled me with fear. I still don't know why she hated me. She let Margaret bully me on many occasions. Becoming fearful and shy made me a target for other bullies."

Molly stood up, reaching for her clothes and started to get ready for school. She went through the same old routine every year. Nothing changed and no one seemed to understand. Fear kept her from reaching out for help.

"Don't be nervous, Darling. There's nothing to fear; it will be like any other school."

"Oh, Mom, how little you know!" Molly thought.

"Hey! My little girl is looking pretty sharp in her new outfit. That band looks beautiful in your hair. Green is definitely your color! Mom adjusted Molly's cute, *Dora the Explorer* backpack. Molly, even though she would be ten in November, loved to watch and listen to the adventures of Dora. She pictured herself becoming a real-life Dora, someday. Mom realized that Molly was shy, and required a lot of encouragement, but felt that this was something that would change as Molly got older. "Go get'em hon!" Mom said, giving Molly a big wink and thumbs-up. Molly smiled weakly.

When kids sensed Molly's insecurity, the teasing would start. She had been teased endlessly since kindergarten about her curly red hair.

"Hey, here comes Little Orphan Annie!"

"Did Daddy Warbucks let you loose?"

"Didn't I see you in the comics? Or maybe it was on *The Simpsons*?

"Watch out for the rabbits, carrot top." This would bring gales of laughter. Molly tried to smile and pretend these comments didn't hurt.

When teams were picked, the most popular people and their friends were chosen first. Then Molly, always last. It was as if they didn't see her. Someone would pipe up and say, "Molly hasn't been chosen yet! She's on your team not mine. I've already got Greg and he's not a very good player!"

They talked about her as if she had no feelings or understanding of what was going on. Decisions made for her never included her opinion. Molly would hear the other girls planning a birthday party or a sleepover with great excitement over the food, the clothes and the presents. Sometimes they were having a magician, or a clown, or going horseback riding out at one of the farms. How she yearned to be included.

Once, Molly overheard one of the girls in her class exclaim, "Don't invite Molly to the party! She's no fun! Nobody likes her! She hardly ever talks!" Molly was deeply hurt by these comments. Parties and sleepovers were things to which she rarely got invitations. Molly pretended she didn't care, but every year it became harder and harder to ignore. Who would be lurking in the playground, or hiding in the classroom, ready to make her life miserable? Would there be another Sara, like in her last school, who never left her alone? Maybe things will be different here.

Even though the weather was warm, Molly felt a chill as she neared the schoolyard. She heard the sounds of children playing, the shouting and the laughter. As she came closer, she could see some kids sitting on the grass chatting, others standing in little groups, some playing catch. All waiting! Everyone was apprehensive about what awaited them, but not in the same way as it was for Molly.

"Hey, you're the new girl that just moved in down the block. What's your name?"

Molly turned towards the voice. A slim, well dressed and very pretty girl, with two other girls who were carbon copies of her, waited for Molly's response. Molly froze! The expression on the girl's face, and in her eyes, was one Molly had seen many times before. Written on each of their Happy Bunny wristbands was 'SCHOOL IS GREAT; THERE'S LOTS OF PEOPLE TO MAKE FUN OF.' For Molly, this was a sign of things to come.

"What's your problem? Cat got your tongue? Maybe a dummy just moved in! Well, aren't you going to answer?" Everyone started to laugh. They appeared to find this girl very funny.

"Speak up," said the girl who was definitely in charge.

"My name is Molly," was the barely whispered acknowledgment.

"I'm Jessica, this is Emily, and this is Mary. We are the most important girls in grade five. We make all decisions around here. We decide who's in and who's out. So far, it doesn't look very promising for you!" Jessica said, laughing at Molly's discomfort.

They all joined arms and raced off across the schoolyard, leaving Molly behind.

"Boy, they must think I'm pretty stupid!" Molly felt disgusted at the way she had handled her introduction to the new girls. "That girl, Jessica, didn't give me a chance," she moaned.

The bell rang. Everyone eagerly raced for the door, trying to be first. Teachers were there with class lists to ensure that everyone got into the proper line, with the proper class, and reached their proper destination.

In the grade five halls, their names had already been placed above hooks where they were to put their coats and book bags. Just as Molly went to hang up her bag, someone pushed into her and she fell against the wall. "Oops! I'm sorry. Your bum was sticking out a bit too far." There was a lot of tittering and muffled giggling at this comment. Molly turned and was staring into the face of none other than Jessica. Molly's face turned red. She lowered her eyes and continued arranging her things. This was no accident. Jessica looked smug.

In the classroom, their names were also on their desks. Molly sat down and looked around her. "Oh! How unlucky can I be?" Jessica was right across from her, Emily was sitting in front of her, and Mary was sitting behind her. This made Molly feel very uncomfortable, as the day with these three girls had not begun very well. Mary and Emily might have been alright, if they hadn't been under the influence of Jessica.

After the National Anthem was played, and the class was seated to listen to announcements, Jessica passed a note to Mary. Mary passed the note on to Emily. Molly tried to ignore what the three were doing but it was almost impossible. Molly knew somehow that the note was about her and Jessica would soon reveal her little secret. When Emily passed the note back to Jessica, Jessica opened it and grinned triumphantly. Making sure that the teacher, Mrs. Murphy, was not watching, Jessica put the note on Molly's desk; then she sat up straight and pretended to be totally absorbed in the teacher's welcoming comments.

Molly looked down at the note. She read:

Do you like the new girl? CHECK yes or no

YES   NO
                    X
                    X

Both Mary and Emily had checked off 'No'. Molly didn't look up; she just shoved the note unto the floor. Jessica grabbed it up quickly so the teacher wouldn't see what she had done. Molly stared at her desk top. Tears stung her eyes.

The first part of the morning was spent on rules, supplies, and how notebooks were to be organized.

The teacher said, "As a class, I want you to come up with a list of good behaviors. At the end of the day, we'll go through the list and you will decide how each was demonstrated during the day, and by whom. The person who accomplishes the best example of good behavior will choose something from the treasure box."

"Get ready for recess. The bell will be ringing in two minutes," said Mrs. Murphy. "The first row ready will be the first to line up." Everyone hurried to be first, but no one beat Jessica.

"Molly, please pay attention! Get ready for dismissal," the teacher said sharply. She had noticed that Molly had not been very attentive this morning.

"Good, Jessica!" exclaimed the teacher. Jessica smiled coyly, with her hands folded primly in front of her.

Molly dreaded going into the yard at recess. She stood against the brick wall, watching the others play. Some were skipping, some playing hopscotch, some sharing their new CD's. Others were just sitting or standing around in little groups, chatting about how the day was progressing so far and catching up on the news from the summer. Molly felt totally left out. Oh, how she wished she belonged to some group, if just for safety's sake.

Jessica and her little entourage sauntered over to where Molly was standing. "How do you like your new school so far, Polly?" Jessica said derisively, knowing very well what she was doing to Molly.

"Molly," whispered Molly, in a timid voice.

Mary and Emily looked uncomfortable. Maybe they were remembering the note.

Mary said, "You live very close to me, Molly. I saw the movers at your house last week."

"So what do you care where she lives? Can't you see she is stupid? Didn't you see her Dorrrra book bag? Duh! How cool is that?" Jessica exclaimed with cunning self-regard and satisfaction. She flipped her long blonde hair from side to side and her blue eyes had a mean glint as she smirked at Molly.

Molly felt that Emily and Mary made an attempt to be friendly, but a fear of Jessica prevented any such thing. Jessica ran off with the other girls trailing her. Emily looked self-consciously at Molly before following after Jessica.

The bell rang. Recess was over. "Thank Heaven!" Molly thought.

As Molly entered the classroom, she saw that the desks were arranged into groups of five. They were going to be given a group assignment in Geography. As each name was already on their desks, it was easy to find their seats.

"Good grief! Look who's in my group: Jessica, Mary, Emily and some boy wearing glasses and looking very serious. Why is this happening!" thought Molly. "With all the people in this class I end up with them!"

"Hi, my name is Paul. I guess you're new here? I was new last year, and for a few days I found it difficult to fit in, not knowing anyone and all. But it's great now."

Molly was pleased to finally hear a pleasant voice. She smiled shyly at Paul. "My name is Molly."

Jessica piped up, "Did you see her Dorrrra book bag in the hall?"

Molly blushed.

"What difference does it make what you carry your books around in? Some people are carrying them in Loblaws bags!" Paul exclaimed in a reproachful manner. "The reason we are in this group, Jessica, is to do an assignment, not to talk about how we carry our books. It's a free world! Molly can carry her books however she chooses. You'd be doing us all a great favor if you worked on your attitude. It stinks!"

"What would you know, Four Eyes?" Jessica sniped, in a voice meant only for Paul.

"Better to see what kind of witch you really are," said Paul in a voice barely audible to anyone except Jessica.

Jessica looked flustered at this rebuke. It was difficult for Molly to conceal her smile. How she wished she could be more like Paul. He wasn't impressed with Jessica. She had no influence over *his* day.

At lunch time, the teacher allowed the students to move the desks around so that they could eat with their friends, as long as they put them back the way they were.

Mary said, "Come and sit here, Molly."

"There is no room here for her. I'm saving it for Sue," Jessica said impatiently.

There were really two empty seats. No one challenged Jessica. Molly pretended that she didn't care and went to sit alone at her own desk. Even though she had brought a great lunch, she had lost her appetite and just played with her food until the bell rang for noon recess. It appeared that Jessica, for some unknown reason, was out to give Molly a hard time. "Bullies don't need reasons," thought Molly.

Coming in after the last recess, Molly's books were knocked off her desk. It happened so quickly that no one noticed that Jessica was to blame. They just thought poor Molly was a klutz. Molly suffered through the rest of the day, receiving continued needling from Jessica. Jessica had found her victim for the year.

When Molly walked through the door at home, Mom came rushing to greet her and gave her a big hug. "How was your day, sweetheart? Come out to the kitchen and tell me all about the new school. I baked your favorite sugar cookies!" Mom said, in a voice filled with pride as she hustled Molly into the kitchen.

"Well?" asked Mom.

"There's not much to tell. It's like every other school I've ever been in," Molly said, trying to hide the tremor in her voice.

"Did you meet anyone you'd like as a friend?" questioned Mom, who was trying hard to hide her concern. Mom knew Molly had difficulty making friends, but each year she hoped things would change. She had no idea how serious the problem was because Molly never said anything.

"There was a boy named Paul in my geography group and he seemed to have a lot of confidence. Everyone liked him. He didn't seem to be influenced by anyone in particular."

It took Molly a long time to go to sleep that night. She tossed and turned, dreaming of monsters with heads like Jessica's, chasing her into a dark forest, where she became entangled in vines and other creepy crawly things, and couldn't get free.

When Molly awoke she didn't feel the least bit rested. Her head hurt and she felt shaky. Nevertheless, she pulled the clothes on that Mom had left hanging over the chair and headed down stairs to the kitchen where she was greeted with a warm, "Good morning, dear!" from Mom.

"Hi, Punkin'!" from Dad. "How's my little girl? Things goin' okay?" He kept his head stuck in the newspaper, sipping his coffee.

Molly couldn't bring herself to tell them how truly horrible her first day had been. To her, it was as though she had been let loose in the jungle, with no weapons to protect herself. She had to keep running and hiding all day to prevent getting seriously injured. At least that's the way it felt. How do I explain to Mom and Dad that no one likes me, as they do? I'm chocolate cake to them and a mud-pie to everyone else.

Molly started down the sidewalk toward the school. As she drew nearer, the shouts of excitement and laughter, rising into the air from the playground, made her freeze. Molly sensed they were waiting for her. She was fresh prey for the predators like Jessica. During her years at school, there had been many Jessicas. The fear she felt was difficult to describe. Molly trembled.

As Molly entered the schoolyard, she saw Jessica standing with a group of girls by the fence near the baseball diamond. Jessica kept looking towards Molly and laughing, and soon a lot of kids were looking at Molly to see what was wrong. Molly looked away. She kept her head down, watching her feet move quickly to the safety of the little corner by the school doors, where she could be out of Jessica's line of vision. Molly had never felt so alone in her life. Jessica was by far the worst offender that she had ever had to deal with. "Likely, as kids get older, they also know how to be meaner," thought Molly.

"Hi, Molly, ready for another day?" said Jessica, putting on an act of friendliness, her eyes betraying her. "You know, Molly, I'm going to have to give you some tips on how to dress. That outfit you're wearing is truly ugly."

Jessica took off with her group as quickly as she had come, leaving Molly alone and very humiliated. Molly wondered if that were why everyone had been laughing at her as she crossed the schoolyard. Molly heard someone say, "You're right! Sure is ugly!" Someone else piped up saying, "Matches her face!" Then lots of gleeful laughter and silly noises filled the air. Molly opened a book, to pretend that she was reading and didn't hear a word of what was said. The pages were nothing but a blur.

As Molly walked down the hall toward her cubby, someone pushed into her from behind. She stumbled but didn't fall. As she passed groups of kids putting their things away, she could hear the muffled sound of suppressed laughter and unintelligible comments being made. She guessed she was the target.

Molly saw Paul coming towards her. She couldn't bear it if he said something mean. When he came up beside her, he reached out and took a sign off Molly's back that read, 'KICK ME I'M UGLY!'

"Looks like the work of Jessica. She's so clever! Someday, she'll get her own," said Paul, smiling down at Molly. "That's a nice outfit you're wearing. Color suits you." Turning, Paul said, "What are you guys gawking at!? Get lost!"

"Thank you Paul," whispered Molly in relief. Molly was surprised at how a few kind words could lift her spirits.

Just before recess, an announcement came over the intercom, "Due to inclement weather, there will be no recess!" Mrs. Murphy said they could get a game, read, write or color, as long as they did it quietly. Molly decided to write in her journal. Before leaving the room, Mrs. Murphy warned them that a teacher was on duty in the hall and would look in every so often. "Be responsible!" she said as she departed.

Molly watched as Jessica inched her way up to the teacher's desk, her eyes darting in every direction to make sure no one was watching. Jessica picked up a duo-tang, opened it, and scribbled something hastily on a little piece of torn paper. Putting the book back, Jessica joined Mary and Emily who were drawing and coloring at their desks. No one else seemed to notice Jessica because they were all absorbed in whatever activity they had chosen for this time.

Molly got up to sharpen her pencil, and as she walked past the teacher's desk, she saw that the duo-tang Jessica had been handling had a label which read, "PERSONAL INFORMA-TION—MRS MURPHY"S CLASS—GRADE 5."

The rest of the day was spent inside. Molly continued to write in her journal. She had decided to document all the things that had happened to her since arriving at her new school. She didn't mention names. Emily, Jessica and Mary were grouped together drawing. Jessica whispered loudly, "Look, Molly" and held up an ugly picture with Molly's name written beneath it. Jessica always made sure no one was watching, except her close friends, when she did these things. As soon as it was seen, Jessica would tear it up and put it in the garbage. Always destroy the evidence. She was so persistent in her astonishing level of cruelty that it was hard to believe she was only ten years old. She seemed to thrive on the reactions of discomfort that she got from her victims.

Molly tried her best to ignore her and added this latest insult to her journal. Along with it, she wrote, "I'm sure someone in this class is trying to start up an 'I Hate Molly Club'."

When the teacher asked questions to involve the class in discussions, Jessica would retreat beneath a surface of sweetness and become the most likeable, darling student in the class. Mrs. Murphy would beam at her intelligent responses. Her written work was superb. Jessica was a remarkable student. She could sure put forth the *sugar and spice and everything nice* image. Molly knew it would be hard to convince any teacher that Jessica was a bully. For the rest of the day, Jessica whispered to others and smiled slyly in Molly's direction.

On dismissal, Molly grabbed her things and hurried home, anxious to avoid any more contact with Jessica or her friends. Though her friends had never initiated any abuse, they condoned it by their silence.

As Molly entered the house, she was wrapped in the loving embrace of her Mom. "I could stay here forever," thought Molly.

"While I finish getting supper ready, why don't you go and start your homework before Dad comes home?" said Mom, as she hurried back to the kitchen. "I'll call you when it's ready."

Molly went into her bedroom and laid out her homework on her desk. She had purposely brought home her journal so she could enter anything else that she might have overlooked. There had to be a way of bringing an end to this harassment.

The phone rang. "Molly, it's for you!" called Mom from the kitchen. "Who would be calling me? No one has my number," thought Molly.

"Hello," Molly said cautiously. There was silence for a minute, then a lot of giggling, laughing, hooting and hollering. Then, in unison, "Molly is a stupid fool! We don't want her at our school!" The receiver was slammed down loudly in Molly's ear. Molly stood for a few minutes in shock and then threw herself down on the bed, burying her face in a pillow, fighting back the urge to cry. "What am I going to do?" said Molly in a tremulous voice. "She is even attacking me in my own home. This is the most frightening thing that has ever happened to me. I can't let her away with this!" Molly lay there until she felt better, then walked over to the desk, sat down, opened her journal and began writing.

Dear Teacher,

I have just come to the end of the worst two days I have ever spent in any school. There is a person in my class who has made my life miserable from the very first minute I set foot in the schoolyard. This person has accomplices, but they only follow; they never do any of the mean things.

Tonight, when I arrived home from school, there was a very nasty phone call for me. How did anyone get my phone number, since it is not yet listed? Today while you were out of the room, I saw this person go up to your desk and copy something from a book labeled 'Personal Information.' I believe it was my telephone number because you are the only one who has it.

On the opposite page, you will find all the things that have happened to me since I moved to this school.

I can't take it anymore.

Molly

The next morning, Molly waited patiently by the corner of the school yard until she saw Paul coming down the street. She knew he was the only one she could trust to do this favor for her. It took every ounce of courage that Molly could muster to confront Paul. She ran to meet him. Molly didn't want anyone to see her, especially Jessica. She said nervously, "Paul, I have something I must do today and I really need your help. Could you please put my journal on Mrs. Murphy's desk? I'll pick it up later today."

"No problem!" said Paul, giving Molly a quizzical look.

Molly gave a sigh of relief and said, "Thanks, I knew I could count on you Paul."

Molly turned quickly and headed away from the school. She couldn't face another day in that place. As the distance between Molly and the school increased, Molly's spirits grew lighter and the tension she had been feeling started to ease.

As Paul stood in the yard waiting for the bell to ring, he couldn't resist the temptation to look in Molly's journal. He wondered why she wanted it put on Mrs. Murphy's desk. He wasn't aware of any homework involving their journals. Paul made an angry remark under his breath as he scanned the two pages written in Molly's neat handwriting. "I knew Jessica was mean, but I never dreamed it would have gone this far! Boy is she going to pay for this!" fumed Paul.

When Paul entered the classroom, he went straight to Mrs. Murphy's desk and placed the journal right in the middle of it so the teacher would have to be blind to miss it.

"Did anyone see Molly this morning?" asked the teacher, as she was checking the attendance. When no one responded, she marked Molly absent. Shortly after the attendance list had been taken to the office, the principal entered the room and spoke quietly to Mrs. Murphy. Turning to the class, he said, "We have a very serious situation on our hands. Try to remember if you saw Molly anywhere near the school this morning. Her mother said she is not at home and there is no reason for her to be absent. She has already notified the police. They will be here sometime this morning to talk to the class."

"Yes, Paul? Did you have something you'd like to tell us?" asked Mrs. Murphy.

Paul stood up and said, "I saw Molly this morning on my way to school. She told me she had something she really had to do today and asked me to put her journal on your desk." Paul walked up to the desk, picked up Molly's journal and handed it to the teacher.

"Oh my goodness!" exclaimed Mrs. Murphy, as she read the journal. "I can't believe something like this could be happening right under my nose and I wouldn't be aware of it. This is terrible! Someone in this class has been treating Molly so badly that she couldn't face coming to school today. That same person was looking through personal information on my desk, copied down Molly's phone number, and gave her a very disturbing phone call last night."

Mrs. Murphy handed the journal to the principal to read. As he read, his frown deepened and his expression became grim. "Whoever has done this is going to pay dearly," he muttered, without even looking at the class. He stamped angrily out of the room.

"I hope whoever is responsible realizes the seriousness of what they have done and will come forward before the end of the day," said Mrs. Murphy. "One way or another, we will get to the bottom of this!"

The class sat in stunned silence. Many turned to look at Jessica as if seeking some kind of confirmation about this situation. Jessica sat fidgeting nervously with her pencil and never looked up. Paul smiled knowingly at Jessica. Emily looked very upset and near tears. Mary was biting on her lower lip as if to prevent saying anything.

When they went into their groups, Paul said to Jessica, "Well, you've gone too far this time. You too, Mary and Emily; you didn't try to stop her! If I were you, I'd go and tell what's been happening to Molly and maybe they'll let you off easy."

"There's nothing to tell," hissed Jessica. "It's her word against ours. Don't listen to him! You'll be sorry if you open your mouth! We didn't do anything. We were just having a bit of fun," said Jessica boldly, but a note of fear had begun to seep into her voice.

Molly heard the squeal of brakes and the loud clash of metal against metal. She jumped nervously and turned toward the noise.

Someone yelled, "You stupid moron! Who taught you to drive, your grandmother?" He obviously didn't think much of grandmothers.

The guy doing the yelling was the one who was in the rear. Molly remembered her father saying, "If you rear-end someone, you are responsible because it shows you weren't in control of your vehicle." This guy's dad obviously forgot to tell him, thought Molly. Boy is he rude!

"Tell it to the cops, when they get here!" yelled the guy who was rear-ended.

The other guy jumped out of his car, waving his arms in a threatening manner. Molly moved quickly away from this scene. "Wow! Why is he so violent, when he is the one who caused the accident?" said Molly in amazement. This reaction left Molly stunned as she trekked along. She had never seen adults act this way.

Molly was really thirsty from all the walking and the warm sun, so she stopped in at a Loblaws store to pick up a bottle of cold water. Just as she reached the checkout for people with eight or fewer items, a woman with a loaded shopping cart pushed her out of the way in a very rude, aggressive manner. Her defiant look was saying, "You're only a kid. You don't count!" Molly wondered if the woman could count.

Molly tried to visualize her mother doing something like this. Just the thought of it made her laugh right out loud. Molly put her water back and left the store. Her first thought was, "That must have been Jessica's mother."

As she left the store and started across the parking lot to the sidewalk, she noticed a man pull into a parking space which read *Pregnant Mothers or Senior Citizens* on the sign beside it. Getting out of the car, he jogged over to the door and disappeared inside. "He's definitely not pregnant and he's not an old man! He jogs, so he doesn't need a space close to the store. What a lazy lout he is!" Molly sighed in disgust. "Maybe he's Jessica's father! Maybe he's morally disabled!" This thought made Molly giggle. She had heard her mother use these expressions and they seemed to apply, even though she wasn't sure of the meaning.

Molly strolled on. For the first time in days, she was feeling some hunger pangs. Taking out her lunch, she glanced around for a nice place to sit and enjoy it. There was a park right across the street, with a bench just begging her to sit. Molly ate her lunch while watching all the activity around her: Baby carriages and strollers being pushed by mothers and grandmothers; pre-school children running, laughing and riding their tricycles.

They had no one to harass them—yet! The adults were very protective of these little treasures. It made Molly feel good just to watch them and listen to their innocent chatter. She had been there, once.

As Molly sat savoring her lunch, she noticed a teenager walking his dog through the park and right next to where the kids were playing. The dog pooed and the boy never stopped to scoop it up. Molly found this disgusting because so many people come into the park to play or have their lunch, as she was doing, and they have to face dog poo. "Ugh! Does he think he is too good to pick up poo? It's his dog!" thought Molly. She was dying to say something to him, but couldn't get up the nerve. "He shouldn't get away with this. How inconsiderate of him! Who does he think he is? There was even a sign on the paved walkway that read, *NO DOGS.* He totally ignored this sign." Molly wondered what it would be like if everyone ignored these signs that were put there for their own protection.

As Molly walked out of the park, she spied a very elderly man toward the back of the city hall and down in a bit of a ravine. He was sitting on a bench, slumped forward, surrounded by cats. Big cats, small cats, thin cats, fat cats, long hair, short hair and every color you could imagine. Molly gasped. She loved cats! "How beautiful is this?" she thought. There were several dishes strewn around the bench, filled with food and water.

"Are these your cats, mister?" said Molly shyly.

"They belong to all of us. They are homeless," the old man said sadly.

"Are you the only one who comes to look after them?" asked Molly.

"There have been several people who donated their time and food. You wonder why some people are so caring, while others are mean and destructive." The old man's eyes filled with tears and his voice was tinged with anger. "It's important to consider peoples feelings."

"I've met people who don't care about my feelings," Molly said, feeling a bit melancholy at the thought.

"What happened here?" Molly asked innocently.

"I built a shelter a few years ago so the cats would be protected from our harsh winter weather. I filled it with straw and put in old blankets and pieces of warm rags for them to sleep on. When I arrived this afternoon, someone had destroyed the shelter. It was kicked to pieces and the contents were strewn all over the hill. Why does someone want to destroy something that is really needed?" said the old man despondently.

"I'm so sorry," Molly said softly. "Could I come and help care for the cats? I'll bring my Dad and he will help you to build the shelters all over again."

"You are a very thoughtful little girl. It would be wonderful if you could help me before the cold weather comes!"

Molly knelt to pet the cats and when she stood up, she said, "I will be back to help rebuild the home for the cats. I promise!"

The old man watched as Molly faded into the distance. He knew she would keep her promise. She was his miracle. He smiled and the anger started to dissolve, as his faith in people was restored.

"My wife had hair like that," he mused.

As Molly headed home she reflected on her day. What a day it had been! Molly had never seen so many rude, angry, destructive, inconsiderate people before. Of course, she had never been out on her own as an observer before. "I feel like a real life Dora," chuckled Molly. "Maybe this is something I should have done long ago. It's certainly opening my eyes to the real world."

Molly thought about the woman who had pushed her aside in line, the man who referred to someone as a "stupid moron" when he was definitely at fault; the teenager in the park who ignored all the rules. Oh, and that man who parked where he shouldn't have. The one ray of sunshine in the whole day was the compassionate old man. What kind of person would destroy something as precious as that shelter, built with love for all those homeless cats? Molly thought about the intimidating Happy Bunny comment on the girls' wristbands. It was cruel! Why did some people try to be so mean? Why is that stuff being sold?

Molly remembered the first time she had ever watched *American Idol* and one of the judges said to a contestant, "You're horrific! Why are you wasting my time? You have absolutely no talent. You certainly don't have the looks of an Idol! You're too fat!" Molly felt so sorry for her that she cried. It took a lot of guts to get up in front of millions of people, then to take being spoken to like that. This judge was all of the people she had seen that day put into one big, unkind lump.

"These programs are attacking people just like me," said Molly out loud. "They're making people feel that it is alright to poke fun at others. Well, it isn't!!" Molly cried. " These are the kind of people who kick over cat shelters and show no consideration for other living things. These are the unbelievably rude people I have witnessed today!"

"There is nothing wrong with me! There is nothing wrong with me! There is nothing wrong with me!" shouted Molly to the world. "I don't deserve to be treated this way. I'm going to stand up to anyone who tries to put me down!" It felt good to shout out loud. Molly stretched her arms up to the sky and did a few pirouettes. She could feel the release of all the tensions and anxieties that had built up over the years fade away.

This new awareness made Molly feel intoxicated. She began to sing out loud…

It's a wonderful day and I'm free,
There's nothing the matter with me.
Wait 'til I tell them, when I get back,
That it isn't me, but something they lack.

A police car pulled up beside Molly.

"Is your name Molly, little girl?" said the policeman in a very serious tone.

"Yes, sir!" said Molly out loud with a great big grin.

"This is not funny," said the officer gruffly. "You've upset a lot of people, little missy!"

"Well then, we're even! A lot of people have upset me!" said Molly, in a voice filled with confidence.

The officer got out and opened the car door. "Get in, Molly; I'm driving you back to school."

When they reached the school, the officer took Molly's hand and led her to the room where her mother and father, her teacher and all her classmates were waiting anxiously.

Molly spoke up right away, so as not giving anyone a chance to reprimand her. "I'm sorry for the trouble I've caused, but I was very upset and needed to get away for awhile. I was trying to understand why there was always someone around to make my life so miserable." Molly choked on these words.

She looked over at Jessica, but Jessica would not meet her eyes.

Molly told them about her adventures. How they made her feel. How she found many rude people out there with no regard for the feelings or welfare of others. She told them the story of the kind old man and the cats. She noticed that some of the children had tears in their eyes when she finished.

Then she turned to Jessica and said, "You had no reason to treat me so meanly. You don't even know me. I'm as good as you and deserve to be shown respect. I'm not going to accept the way you've been treating me any longer! You sneaked around and even got my phone number so you could harass me in my own home. I saw you going through the teacher's book. Please don't deny it."

Jessica's face turned red. She looked around the class to get a show of support. She was confronted by a stony silence. "There were others who were doing the same thing!" spluttered Jessica. "Mary and Emily were always with me—they knew what was going on. They are as much to blame as I am!"

"I don't agree with that," said Molly. "The others just followed you because they were afraid of what you would do to them if they said anything."

Molly turned to the class and said, "I learned a lot about people today. The things I observed will always be with me. We must stand up to people who bully and if we are witness to any form of bad behavior, we'll do something about it! It's important to become sensitive to the way we are making other people feel. I know what it's like to spend my day with you feeling lonely and rejected. I always felt that somehow I was responsible for the way that I was being treated. It intimidated me and I couldn't defend myself. While I wandered around town today, I realized that there was something strong inside of me, like a little voice that said "Molly you can do it! Stop feeling sorry for yourself." It was then that I understood that it was up to me to change things. I will never again allow anyone to abuse me, or anyone else, if I can help it!"

"Mom and Dad, thanks for always being there," said Molly, with love in her voice.

Molly raised her voice and said, "No longer! Yes Siree! There is nothing wrong with me!"

The class cheered, "Way to go, Molly!"

Paul put his arm around Molly's shoulders and said, "By golly, Molly, you're right!"

The intercom came on and the principal said in a stern voice, "Please send Jessica to the office right away!"

Everyone in the classroom turned to look at Jessica. Jessica's face was flushed and she was looking very nervous. With her head down and her shoulders hunched she scurried to the door and out as quickly as possible to avoid the looks of disbelief and disapproval on the faces of her peers...Some people she had bullied showed her no sympathy, while some, including Molly, were able to empathize with her situation. She and Molly had just changed roles. Now Molly was the one who held the true power and the support of her peers.

Mrs. Murphy shook her head in disbelief and said, "I'm so sorry, Molly. I hope no one will allow something like this to ever happen again."

Molly's Mom and Dad rushed forward and embraced her in a big bear hug. "Oh Molly, you can't believe how relieved we are that you are safe," they cried in unison.

Molly's Mom turned to Mrs. Murphy saying, "I was unaware that Molly was having a problem of this nature. It really hurts me that she found school an unsafe and unhappy place and felt that telling us would only lead to more harassment. I hope we can get together and discuss setting up a parental awareness campaign so this type of thing never happens again. Molly, I am so proud of how you handled this!"

"You can be sure that we will do everything possible to see

that nothing like this ever occurs again," said Mrs. Murphy, still shaking her head in disbelief.

Many of the children raised their hands, wanting to express their feelings to Molly.

"It is a good thing that Molly got to speak up and let everyone know how she felt. I had no idea what she was going through and I think that only a few of us did," said Sara

"I definitely don't think it's fair for someone to wake up in the morning and not want to go to school because of fear or that they will be made fun of," said Henry turning to Molly. "Sorry Molly! School is hard enough without all this."

Another hand was waving in the air. "Yes Megan?" said the teacher.

"Bullying is not fair because it makes people feel bad about themselves. I feel so sorry that I wasn't there for you, Molly!"

Mary's hand went up slowly. She appeared uncomfortable. "Molly, I would have been nicer to you except I was afraid of Jessica. I now know that is not a good reason. I'm sorry."

Nearly everyone in the class expressed their feelings. Molly's smile was radiant.

"Remember I told you about the old man who was looking after all the stray cats that didn't have homes and someone came along and vandalized his shelters? Well I promised that I would return with my father and help him construct the shelters again before winter sets in. If there is anyone who is able to take part in this excursion I'd be mighty happy," said Molly eagerly.

Paul stepped forward right away. "I'd love to Molly! It's for such a worthwhile cause."

Soon there were many offers. Molly told them to collect old towels, rags and anything else that would make a nice warm lining for the cat's houses. Several kids threw in great suggestions for making these homes deluxe. Some of the suggestions were really laughable.

"Let's make the buildings two-stories high and have a family room where they can all go to get to know one another better," said Beth.

"We could have people knit sweaters for the cats for the real cold days. I think my Grandma would love to do that," said Emily. "Couldn't you just picture a bunch of cats running around in pretty colored sweaters?"

"Blue for the boys and pink for the girls," spouted Kevin with a big smile.

"How about constructing an outhouse for the cats? I have one at my cottage and it works great," Charley said with a huge grin.

"Let's get someone to wire the shelters for heat and light! Maybe my Dad would do it, he's an electrician." Angela looked so serious about her suggestion that the class laughed until they cried.

Everyone had a good time over the silly comments that were made, but some of the ideas were great and would soon be put to the test.

Molly's Dad got his tools and some old lumber, and insulation he had in the garage, and with the children headed down to the ravine back of the city hall. All the children had brought their offerings and were ready and anxious to help. It made them feel great that they were participating in such a worthwhile project.

When they pulled in and parked at the sight, all the children squealed with delight when they saw the beautiful cats. They scrambled out of the van with their collected treasures and hurried over to the place where the old man was sitting. He looked up and the first person he saw was Molly. She put out her hand and he grasped it in both of his, beaming from ear to ear. "I knew you would keep your promise!" he said adoringly.

Molly's father and the children worked hard all afternoon. Soon the shelters were up. They were not only sturdier than the old ones but the children had painted them every color of the rainbow. They felt if they made them really beautiful the vandals would even appreciate them.

The old man watched with admiration as the final touches were made and everyone was getting ready to depart. He beckoned them to come close,

"This has been a true act of love. You'll never know how much it has meant to me. No one ever gave me a gift as great as this. I want you all to remember that a simple act of kindness can change the whole world."

"We'll all be back to make sure things go well," said Molly's father, his voice filled with emotion. "Right kids?"

"You bet!" they chorused.

On the drive back Molly thought about all the things that had happened to her in so short a time. "By golly, I think I've found the old Molly!" she said with conviction. "Maybe Dora inspired me a little." Molly put her head back and closed her eyes. A happy smile tugged at the corners of her mouth.

Paul, who was sitting across from Molly, said, "Molly I think you have become your own hero!"

All the schools in town are filled to capacity. The classrooms are warm and welcoming (at least we hope they are) and crackling with the energy of the young. Molly has become the leader of the most important group of girls in grade five. To Molly they are all important.

Don't Let the Bullies Bully You

Don't let the bullies
Bully you!
Take them to task,
And when you are through,
Put up a sign
For the world to see,
"There's no one better
Than you or me."
My skin may be different,
My hair and my size.
I may wear glasses,
Which cover my eyes.
I eat to survive,
I cry when I'm sad,
And just like you,
I smile when I'm glad.
We're only divided
By what's in our heart;
It's the one thing
That might keep us apart.
Love
Molly

EPILOGUE

If you see some child alone and fearful in the schoolyard, being taunted or teased, like Molly was, go to them and say something kind then report the incident. Don't just be bystanders!

Remember this old Irish Proverb—"There is no need like the lack of a friend."